THE LITTLE REINDEER

For my wife, Louise, who told me about the Little Reindeer.

First published in the United States 1997 by
Dial Books for Young Readers
A Division of Penguin Books USA Inc.
375 Hudson Street
New York, New York 10014

Published in Great Britain 1996 by
Andersen Press Ltd
Copyright © 1996 by Michael Foreman

First Edition
1 3 5 7 9 10 8 6 4 2

Library of Congress Cataloging in Publication Data
Foreman, Michael, date.
The little reindeer/written and illustrated
by Michael Foreman.—1st ed.
p. cm.
Summary: A young reindeer becomes
a surprise Christmas gift for a city boy.
ISBN 0-8037-2184-6 (trade)
[1. Reindeer—Fiction. 2. Christmas—Fiction.] I. Title.
PZ7.F7583Li 1997 [E]—dc20 96-27128 CIP AC

The
Little Reindeer

written and illustrated by

Michael Foreman

Dial Books for Young Readers

New York

The little reindeer wondered what all the fuss was about.
He could see lights blazing in the windows of the snow-
covered buildings. Shadowy figures rushed in and out of
the doorways carrying mysterious bundles.

The little reindeer picked his way through deep snow toward the biggest building. As he got closer he could hear singing and banging, whirring and rustling.

The little reindeer peeked around the door into the warm, noisy room.

Amazing animals were streaming between rows of singing people. The little reindeer moved farther into the room and found himself being carried along with the rest of the animals.

He tried to back away, but was pushed forward
by the animals pressing from behind. Suddenly
they all disappeared in a blizzard of colored paper.

He was turned over and over in swirling colors. Then it went black and cold and things bumped down on him until he couldn't move.

He heard jingling bells and
cheering, and felt a big whoosh.

For hours they seemed to stop and start and swoop up and
down, until the little reindeer was tumbling head over hoofs again.

He tried to move his legs, and managed to stand up. He was relieved to feel the softness of snow beneath his hoofs, but he still couldn't see anything. The little reindeer stood in the darkness, surrounded by strange sounds. Then he heard footsteps crunching toward him.

Suddenly he found himself staring at an astonished face, and a smile.

"Wow! What a present!" The boy picked him up and danced around and around in the snow.

"But where can I keep you? There are no pets allowed in the building....I know, you can stay up here with my pigeons."

The boy opened the door of a large shed at one end of the roof. Immediately the sky filled with birds.

In a corner of the shed
the boy made a straw bed for
the reindeer and brought milk
and four kinds of cereal.
"Tomorrow we can try different things to
eat and see what you like best."
Two by two the pigeons returned to the
shed. They didn't seem to mind the new
visitor at all.

Each day the boy brought food and milk.
The reindeer liked peanut butter sandwiches
best of all. While the pigeons flew higher
and higher in the sky, the boy and the
reindeer strolled around the roof and watched
the busy city life below.

The weather gradually grew warmer
and the little reindeer grew bigger.
  One day when the boy opened the
door to let out the pigeons, the reindeer
flew out with them.

The reindeer didn't fly far
that first time, just across to the
neighboring building and back.
But as the days passed, he flew
farther and farther.
   The boy was overjoyed.
He had told no one about
his wonderful Christmas pet
because he knew he would not
be allowed to keep him.

By early summer the reindeer was big enough to give the boy rides around the roof. Then, one evening, they flew together over the roofs of the city.

When the first snowflakes of
winter began to fall, the boy noticed
a look of sadness in the reindeer's
eyes. The boy hugged him as always,
but the reindeer looked up at the
swiftly moving gray clouds and
sighed.

The boy knew that the reindeer had to go back to his real home. He knew his reindeer was going to be one of the few chosen to carry a sleigh full of presents across the night skies.

On Christmas Eve the boy gave the reindeer his favorite dinner, and the pigeons sang. They were still singing when he kissed the reindeer good night.

From his bed, just as he started to dream,
the boy thought he heard jingling bells.

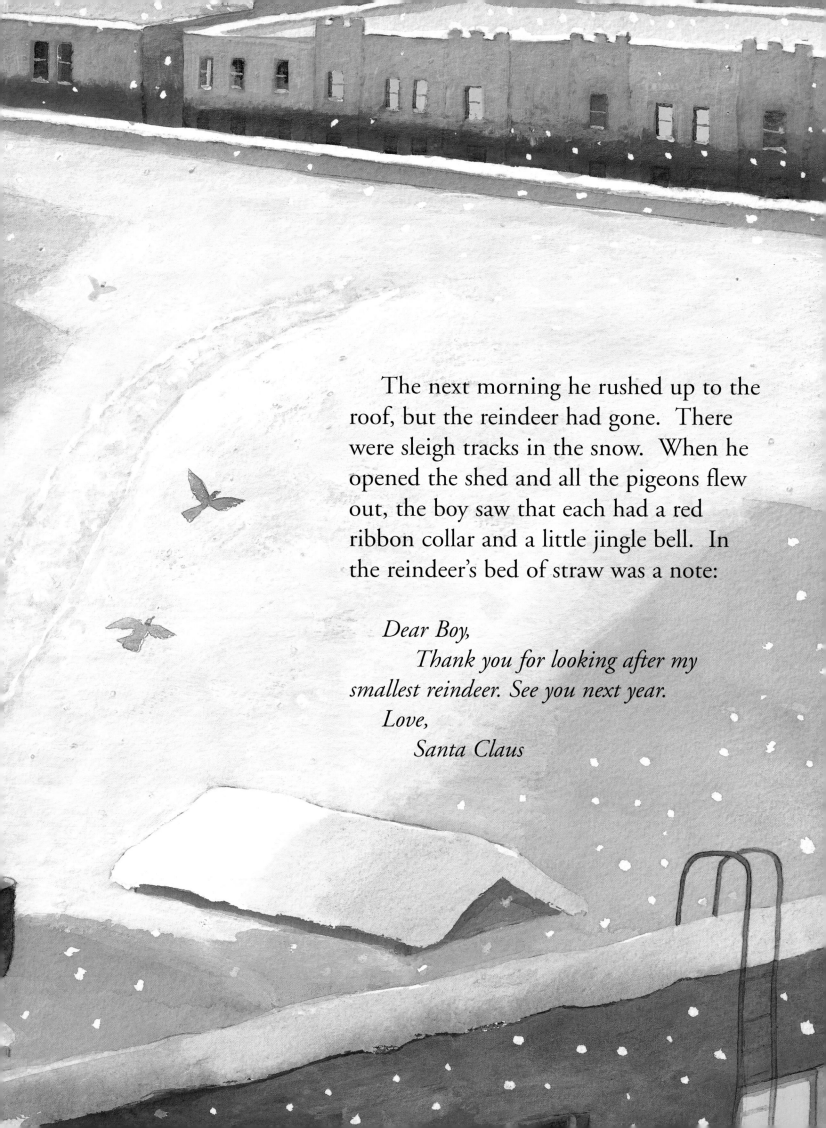

The next morning he rushed up to the roof, but the reindeer had gone. There were sleigh tracks in the snow. When he opened the shed and all the pigeons flew out, the boy saw that each had a red ribbon collar and a little jingle bell. In the reindeer's bed of straw was a note:

Dear Boy,
     Thank you for looking after my smallest reindeer. See you next year.
Love,
     Santa Claus

Through the next spring, summer, and autumn the boy
heard the tinkling and jingling of bells each time the pigeons
flew. And on Christmas Eve, when he heard the real jingle
bells coming down from the snowy sky, he was waiting on
the roof with milk and peanut butter sandwiches.